For Ben and Mary Courson,
two of my favorite readers.

Ideals Children's Books • Nashville, Tennessee

Published by Ideals Children's Books
An imprint of Hambleton-Hill Publishing, Inc.
Nashville, Tennessee 37218

Printed and bound in the United States of America

Library of Congress Cataloging-in-Publication Data

Hallinan, P.K.
    Just open a book / written and illustrated by P.K. Hallinan.
        p.   cm.
    Summary: Rhymed text and illustrations describe the many adventures
one can find in books.
    ISBN 1-57102-027-6 (lib.)—ISBN 1-57102-015-2 (pbk.)
    [1. Books and reading—Fiction. 2. Stories in rhyme.] I. Title.
PZ8.3.H15Jv   1995
    [E]—dc20   94-31994
                                                                     CIP
                                                                     AC

Just open a book
and begin to read through
the world of enjoyment
that's waiting for you.

You can take a long trip
on an old pirate ship,

or walk in the sand

where the pyramids stand.

You can go to the moon
and then, if you please,
you can see for yourself
if it's made of green cheese.

Just open a book—
it's all you need do
to make your most fabulous
wishes come true.

or great dinosaurs . . .

or fly with an eagle
and learn how it soars.

What else is in books?

Just take a good look.

Paul Bunyan is waiting
for someone like you
to ask him why Babe,
his pet ox, is blue.

And young Johnny Appleseed
sure needs a hand
planting his seedlings
all over the land.

With books you can travel
and easily greet
all of the people
you've wanted to meet.

In foggy old London
it's certain that you
can help Sherlock Holmes
solve a mystery or two.

Tom Sawyer is building
a raft with Huck Finn.
As soon as you get there,
the voyage will begin.

You can walk through a wood
with your friend Robin Hood,

or have a nice feast
with Beauty and the Beast.

And, if you like,
you might even choose
to find out why Big Foot
can't wear any shoes.

Yes, books are a way
to enjoy every day.

So next time you think you've got nothing to do, just look at the books that were written for you.

or even to cook.

It's easy if you'll . . .